and the Mysteries of the Universe

Books about Cody

Cody

and the Mysteries of the Universe

TRICIA SPRINGSTUBB

illustrated by
ELIZA WHEELER

CANDLEWICK PRESS

Text copyright © 2016 by Tricia Springstubb
Illustrations copyright © 2016 by Eliza Wheeler

First paperback edition 2017

Library of Congress Catalog Card Number 2014960101
ISBN 978-0-7636-5858-8 (hardcover)
ISBN 978-0-7636-9453-1 (paperback)

17 18 19 20 21 22 BVG 10 9 8 7 6 5 4 3 2 1

Printed in Berryville, VA, U.S.A.

This book was typeset in Dante.
The illustrations were done in ink and watercolor.

Candlewick Press
99 Dover Street
Somerville, Massachusetts 02144

visit us at www.candlewick.com

For Zoe and Andy
T. S.

For my cousin and bosom friend, Greta
E. W.

1
Welcome!

In this life, many things are hard to wait for:

Your turn

Your birthday

Being allowed to get a real tattoo

But if Cody had to name the hardest thing of all, it would be waiting for her best friend, Spencer.

This was not ordinary waiting. This was big-time waiting. Because Spencer wasn't just coming for a visit, like usual. He was coming for good! He was moving in with his grandmother, right around the corner. It was Cody's dream come true.

Except where was that boy, anyway?

Cody waited with Spencer's grandmother, otherwise known as GG, on GG's front porch. They'd made a WELCOME sign. They'd baked Spencer's favorite cookies: mucho chocolate chips, zero nuts.

Everything was at the ready.

Cody squinted toward the corner. She petted GG's cat, MewMew. MewMew was deaf, so Cody did cat sign language for "Any minute now!"

She did all this six gazillion times. Give or take.

"Patience is a virtue." GG cleaned her glasses on her T-shirt. She put them back on, and then she squinted toward the corner, too.

Still no Spencer.

Maybe their car broke down. Or they got lost. Maybe his parents changed their minds and decided not to move here after all. A cloud of worry threw its dark shadow over Cody.

"Don't worry." GG was a teacher. She could read minds.

Cody tried her best to un-worry. She looked around the front porch, which was an interesting place. GG lived in a side-by-side. Her side had flower-pots and wind chimes. It had a swing with comfy tie-dye pillows.

The other side had a rusty chair and a plant that was dying of thirst. Taped to the window was a skull-and-crossbones flag. The name on the mailbox was MEEN.

So far, Cody had never seen a Meen. Which is a poem!

Also a mystery. Who were the Meens? Were they pirates out sailing the high seas? Vampires who feared the light? Or just extremely shy people?

Life holds many mysteries. Cody planned to solve this one. Just as soon as Spencer got here to help.

Squint, squint, squint.

Pet, pet, pet.

Sigh, sigh, sigh.

Whoa!

A car pulling a trailer turned the corner. GG and Cody rocketed off the porch.

One big hugging festival, that's what they all had.

Good old Spencer looked just the same—irresistible curls, round face, and thick glasses. He and Cody did their special, secret ant greeting. When ants meet, they touch feelers. That is ant for "So glad to see you, old buddy!" Now Spencer and Cody touched

foreheads and gave a little rub-a-dub-dub. One of the many important things Cody had taught Spencer was to admire ants.

The trailer was packed from top to bottom. Spencer's father, Mr. Pickett, looked from the trailer to GG's little house and back again. He scratched his head.

"Don't worry," said GG, Reader of Minds. "Everything will fit. Love always fits! It's a scientific fact."

Everyone started pulling boxes out of the trailer. Cody reached for an interesting-shaped case.

"Careful!" Spencer said in a voice of alarm.

"I'm always careful."

"Not always," he said. "Not in my experience."

Careful was Spencer's middle name. Cody was more of an action person, herself.

"What's in that case, anyway?" she said. "Gold doubloons? A tiny mummy?"

"My violin."

"Really?" Cody was impressed. "You never told me you play the violin."

"Yes, I did."

"No, you didn't."

"You just forget."

"Me?" Impressed turned into insulted. "I never forget stuff!"

"Sometimes you do. In my experience."

Whew. Cody had forgotten how difficult this boy could be.

No, she hadn't! She never forgot stuff!

"Cody." GG put an arm around her. She whispered in Cody's ear. "Spencer's had a long day. Poor pumpkin's tuckered out and a little cranky. Why don't you say good-bye and come back tomorrow?"

Good-bye? Tomorrow? This was not the plan. What about solving the mystery? What about eating the cookies?

"Remember," GG whispered. "Patience is a virtue."

If Cody was in charge of the English language, that word would go right out the window.

2
Mr. Meen

Patience. The next morning, Cody gave it a try.

First she patiently practiced eating cereal right-handed. She patiently helped Mom choose her outfit for work. Mom was Head of Shoes at O'Becker Department Store, and appearances were very important.

After Mom left, she patiently fed toast crusts to the ants in the front yard and sang them "You Are My Sunshine." The ants loved this song, which was her and Dad's favorite. Back inside, she patiently counted the calendar for how many days till Dad, who was a trucker, got home. Too many, as usual. She even read a whole chapter of her boring summer reading book.

Almost a whole chapter.

Patience really took it out of you. When she couldn't wait one second longer, Cody ran upstairs to her big brother Wyatt's room. He was still asleep, of course. Wyatt was a genius, so his brain required extra rest.

Wyatt's room was fascinating. Mom said someday she was going to call in archaeologists to do an excavation. Cody took the opportunity to examine some of his if-you-touch-this-you-die stuff. She dug through the piles of clothes on the floor and selected the T-shirt he got at doctor camp. I ♥ BLOOD AND GUTS, it said. She pulled it on. It smelled like Wyatt's anti-pimple soap.

"I'm going to GG's," she said. "Spencer and I are going to spy on the Meens. Want to come?"

Wyatt flopped his skinny arm around.

"Is that a yes?" Cody asked patiently.

"Three days till school," he said in his computer voice. "Must maximize sleep."

School? Already? This was the problem with summer vacation. First it was like a beautiful blue sea. You sailed along, having wonderful adventures. You were free as a dolphin! Happy as a mermaid! You forgot all about life on shore and then *clunk!* Your boat hit a rock. The voyage was over.

"Are you sure?"

"My data is always accurate," said Computerized Wyatt.

"Then there's no time to waste. *Adiós, amigo.*"

Cody loved the in-between times of day, like now, when morning slipped into afternoon. Her neighbor, wearing a hat shaped like a flying saucer, was digging in the garden. Her baby sat in the grass, licking a Popsicle. A little brown dog licked the baby's knee. Everyone waved to Cody — well, not the dog. Any other day, she'd stop for a chat. But today she had a mission.

A truck was just pulling up in front of GG's. On the side was a picture of a beetle with its legs in the air and Xs for eyes. BIG OR SMALL, WE GET THEM ALL, it said.

A man climbed out. He was so tall, he had to unfold himself like a beach chair. His beard was wild and red. His big boots clomped across the grass, up the front steps, and through the Meen door.

A Meen! Cody had finally seen a Meen!

She raced up the steps and knocked on GG's door. When Spencer came out, he did some blinking, like a boy still surprised to be here.

"Guess what?" Cody said. "I saw Mr. Meen! He's got muscles on top of muscles."

Spencer sat down on the swing. His curls were perky on one side but smushed on the other.

"Also," said Cody, "he's a cold-blooded murderer."

Spencer's eyes went wide. Cody sat beside him and started up the swing.

"A *bug* murderer," she said.

"Oh. Whew." Spencer looked relieved. "Bugs. That's different."

Cody stopped that swing cold. *Plonk* went Spencer's head against the back.

"Would you like it if a bug said that about you? Oh. Whew. A human. That's different." She crossed her arms. "Murder is murder."

Usually Spencer liked to argue. He called it debating. But today he just rubbed his plonked head. When he finally spoke, it was in a voice of quiet.

"School starts in three days," he said. "I won't know where the bathrooms are. I won't know where to put my jacket. I won't know any kids."

And he said *she* forgot things! Poor Spencer. Cody started the swing up again. Nice and slow this time, the way he liked.

"You'll know me. We won't be in the same class, but I'll take care of you."

Spencer stopped frowning. Cody made the swing go a tiny bit faster.

"I'll teach you which lunch ladies are nice. And which water fountain tastes disgusting. I'll introduce you to my friend Pearl. I already told her all about you."

Like sun slowly peeping from behind a cloud, that was Spencer's smile.

"Everything will be perfect," Cody told him.

But then a terrible thought made her stop the swing so fast, both their heads hit the back. *Plonk plonk.*

"I mean. Unless . . ."

"Unless what?"

"Never mind." Cody tried to start swinging again, but Spencer put his foot down.

"You have to tell me!"

"Unless . . . you get the Spindle."

"The Spindle! Is that a teacher? Is she really mean? She sounds really, really mean."

This was the wrong road to go down.

"Let's not talk about school." Cody poked his smushed curls to perk them up. "It's not for three whole days. Anyway, speaking of mean, want to spy on Mr. Meen?"

Spencer took forever to decide things, even no-brainers like spying on a murderer.

Cody waited. Patience is a virtue, after all.

Also, patience is a pain in the neck.

"Sure you do!" She grabbed his hand. "Come on."

3
Spies

They crouched under the skull-and-crossbones window.

"You keep watch," Cody whispered.

"For what?" Spencer whispered.

"In case Mr. Murderer Meen rushes out."

Spencer crawled away backward. *Crawl crawl crawl*, right under the swing.

"I can watch from here," he whispered.

Holding her breath, Cody peeked over the window ledge. Mr. Meen lay asleep on a couch. His cap was over his eyes. His mouth hung open. Whoa! Were those gold teeth? Cody flattened her hands on the window ledge to get a better look.

A fiery dagger stabbed her palm.

"Oh! Ow, ow!"

An angry yellow jacket shot up in front of her. In all of the insect kingdom, yellow jackets were Cody's last favorite. This one zigged and zagged, aiming toward Spencer.

"No! Help!" He tried to get away and bumped his head on the swing. "Ow! No!"

"What's going on?" The Meen door swung wide. "Somebody getting murdered out here?"

A useful thing to know—yellow jackets are not scared of anybody. Not even men with pirate beards and muscles on top of muscles, who just got woken up from their naps and are not in what you'd call a good mood.

That fearless, foolish yellow jacket flew straight at Mr. Meen. He crashed his big hands together like cymbals. *Smack!* With a face of disgust, he dusted that very dead yellow jacket onto the floor.

"Bugs!" he growled. "If I never see another one, it'll be too soon."

He turned on his heel and clomped back inside.

Spencer crawled out from under the swing. He and Cody stared at her hand.

"Oh no! It stung you two times!" Spencer looked ready to faint. "Are you allergic? Stings can be fatal."

Cody's knees began to wobble. Tears spurted into her eyes. The red bumps on her hand hypnotized her. She could not stop looking at them. If it wasn't for Spencer, she might have stood there frozen forever. But her friend opened the door and led her inside.

"Poor pumpkin!" cried GG. She was making biscuits. She wiped Cody's wet cheeks with a floury finger, then examined her hand. "That's just a local reaction," she said. "You'll be fine. I'll disinfect it."

Cody tried for a face of courage. This was hard, because her salty tears and GG's flour had pasted her cheeks together.

It got even harder when GG took out an unfriendly-looking brown bottle that said HYDRO-something.

"Be brave," whispered Spencer. He rubbed his forehead against hers. *You can do it, buddy!*

Cody squinched her eyes. Something cool and wet swiped her hand.

"All done!" said GG.

Cody opened her eyes. The red bumps were still there, but she felt better.

"That yellow jacket was so little," she said. "How could it hurt so much?"

"Small things can pack a big punch." GG hugged both of them. "That goes for the two of you!"

GG wrapped up some of the special welcome cookies, and some warm biscuits, and some tomatoes and green beans from her garden. By the time Cody left, she had a big grocery bag.

Mr. Meen was on the porch drinking soda pop. His boots were propped up on the railing. Those boots had steel tips. An ant would get a heart attack just looking at those boots.

"Here." He held out a jar. "You're going to itch like a flea-bit dog. Better take this."

"Thank you," said Cody.

She watched Mr. Meen crush the soda can in his fist. As fast as a girl clutching a mysterious jar and a big bag of groceries can run, that's how fast she ran home.

4
Eyes Do Not Wear Clothes

"The murderer who lives next door to GG gave me this." Cody showed Wyatt the jar. *Big Ralph's Meat Tenderizer,* said the label.

"Meat tenderizer? A murderer gave you meat tenderizer?" He read the ingredients. Mom always did that, to make sure there weren't too many chemicals. But Wyatt adored chemicals.

"Dextrose," he read. "Calcium silicate. Bromelain. That's an enzyme."

Wyatt explained all about enzymes. Explaining

things that are very boring is how a genius is nice to you.

"The enzyme will help break down the yellow-jacket poison," he said. *"Excelente."*

Wyatt mixed the tenderizer with water, then spread the paste over Cody's hand. Gentle as a bedtime kiss, that's how his touch was.

"You're going to be the world's best doctor," Cody said.

Wyatt laughed. His nice laugh, not the other one.

He had a microscope slide of a bee stinger, and he let Cody examine it. Through the lens, the stinger looked mighty as a sword. That made Cody feel bad. That poor yellow jacket! He only meant to defend himself. But he wound up deader than dead.

Wyatt got another slide and squeezed some puddle water onto it. He explained that the golden blobs were mosquito eggs. Those squiggly things were bacteria, very-very-very-you-get-the-idea-tiny creatures.

"A puddle contains a whole, entire universe," he told her. "And it's all invisible to the naked eye."

That cracked Cody up. Like eyes ever wore clothes! Imagine an eyeball with a bow tie and a little top hat!

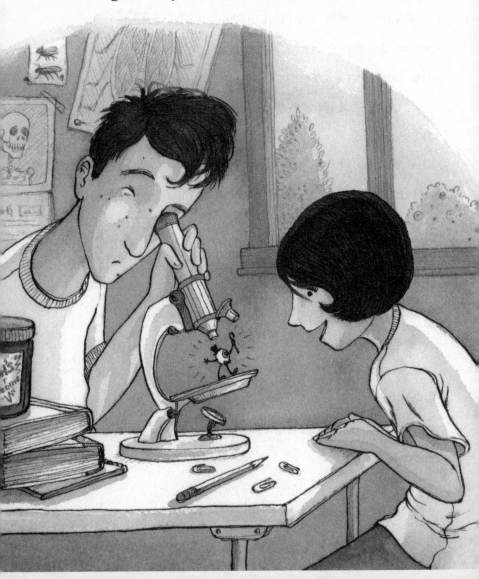

Somewhere in the room, Wyatt's cell phone began to ring. The two of them hurled around underwear, books, shoes, and dirty dishes. At last, Cody poked her head under the bed and ta-da!

"You have reached the office of Dr. Wyatt," she said. "If this is an emergency, dial nine-one-one immediately."

"Cody! What are you doing with your brother's phone?"

Cody recognized the voice of Payton Underwood, the girl of Wyatt's dreams. Or, in Cody's opinion, his nightmares.

"We are busy with other customers. Please try again later. Maybe in three years."

Wyatt grabbed the phone. "Payton? Sorry!" He rushed out of the room.

Cody sat on her brother's bed. Sometimes a person just wants to give another person a present, even if it's not their birthday or Christmas. A present for no reason except you like them so much. But what could she give Wyatt?

Cody had a friendly brain. When an idea knocked, her brain said, *Come in, idea. Make yourself right at home.* And what do you know? *Knock, knock.* Here came one now!

First she found a clean slide. Then she worked up a great, gobby mouthful of spit. If you are thinking disgusting, you are right. But if you are thinking fun, you are also right. How can that be? In this life, many things can stump the mind.

When she had so much spit she could hear it sloshing around, Cody drooled on the slide.

"What are you doing?" hollered Wyatt.

Oops! The slide spurted from Cody's hand. It landed on Wyatt's desk. Spit side down. She tried to pick it up, but spit is highly slippery stuff.

"You drooled on my scientific equipment!" Wyatt smacked his forehead. "How can you be my sister? How can we share the same DNA?"

"What does that spell?"

"Never mind!"

"I was making a new slide," she said. "So you could examine the universe of my spit!"

"It's not spit. It's *saliva*." Wyatt dive-bombed his bed. "And it's swarming with bacteria, viruses, and fungi!"

That gave Cody a better-sit-down-on-the-bed feeling. But Wyatt ordered her off. Pronto.

How could he be nice to her one minute and mean the next? There was only one explanation.

"Payton Underwood broke up with you again, didn't she?" she asked.

"None of your business!"

"I knew it. That no-good, rotten P.U."

Wyatt stuck his head under his pillow. He needed somebody to rub tender circles on his back, like Mom did when they were sad. Cody knew this, but Wyatt didn't. Sometimes even geniuses get confused. He pointed at the door. *Adiós!*

Cody trudged out. A dribble of drool still clung to her chin. She wiped it off and examined it. But no matter how she looked, no swarms of bacteria, viruses, or fungi were visible. Not to her naked eye.

It made a person wonder. What other invisible stuff was out there?

5
Into Thin Air

No matter how much Big Ralph's she used, Cody's hand itched like a flea-bit dog. Wyatt the Miserable said yellow-jacket poison was seeping through her blood. Does that sound like a helpful remark?

The night before school started, Mom came home from work and told Cody to have a seat on the couch. Cody made happy toes. Mom had picked out four pairs of new school shoes, and she got to choose two.

"The camouflage high-tops are cute and practical," Mom said. "But how about these Mary Janes? Notice the detailing on the buckles."

In the end, Cody picked the sparkly purple boots and the polka-dot sneakers.

"You sure those boots don't pinch?" said Mom.

"They're perfecto!"

"Oh, madam," said Mom, "if only all my customers possessed your exquisite taste and manners!"

After supper, Cody and Mom strolled over to GG's house. It wasn't dark yet, but the streetlights came on as if they couldn't wait to do their job. The evening air was warm on top but chilly on the bottom. Cody's head was still in summer, but her feet were already in autumn.

GG's windows shone bright and cheerful. The Meen windows were dark. And what was this? The skull-and-crossbones sign was gone. In its place was a WELCOME HOME sign. The Os were cute little hearts.

Cody studied the sign with eyes of admiration. Who had made it? And welcome home who?

She gave her flea-bit hand a thoughtful scratch. The mystery deepened.

GG's house was always cozy. Now that three extra people lived there, it was cozy to the max. Boxes filled the hallway. MewMew, Queen of Box Mountain, perched on top. Lucky duck Spencer got to sleep on the couch in a sleeping bag, like camping out every night.

He was getting ready to practice his violin. Mom and Cody sat down to listen. The song he played was called "Go Tell Aunt Rhody." The music was complicated. Was it sad? Was it happy? Could it be both at the same time? Cody decided it was perfect night-before-school music. All the while he played, her hand un-itched.

When he took a bow, she and Mom clapped their heads off. Mom gave him a kiss, then squeezed her way down the hall to the kitchen, where the grown-ups were.

"I could feel that music inside me," Cody told

Spencer. "It seeped right through me, like yellow-jacket poison, only nice."

Up till now, Cody's favorite instrument had been drums, but people are allowed to change their minds. If only Spencer would let her try his violin! But he was already putting it away. Carefully. First he wiped it with a special cloth. Then he fit it into the red-velvet-lined case. He unscrewed the bow. *Snap snap, zip zip.*

At last he looked at Cody.

"School called today." His voice was the size of a mosquito egg. "I got the Spindle."

Oh, no. Quiet, sensitive Spencer. He'd be no match for Mrs. Spindle. He was going to need Cody's help more than ever. Starting right now.

"Let's not waste our last drop of vacation," she said. "Let's just forget about school."

"That's impossible."

"I don't mean *really* forget. I mean . . . oh, never mind! Let's practice our spying on the grown-ups."

Down the hall they crept, past the boxes, and a slumpy pile of winter coats, and Mr. Pickett's golf clubs. MewMew came, too. Here is a tip: to learn how to be an excellent spy, just observe a cat.

In the kitchen, the grown-ups sat at the table talking.

"Our own start-up," Mr. Pickett was telling Mom.

"It won't be easy," Mrs. Pickett said.

"In this economic climate," Mr. Pickett said.

"My parents are starting a new business," Spencer whispered to Cody. "Their old one fizzled."

"It'll work out," GG said. "Just remember.
Patience is a virtue."

Mrs. Pickett had irresistible curls to match Spencer's. She tossed her head and laughed.

"Mother," she said, "if I had a dollar for every time
you told me that, I'd be a millionaire!"

That cracked Cody up.

Which made her topple sideways.

Ditto the bag of golf clubs.

Thus ended their spy mission.

• • •

Just before bed, Dad called from the road. Cody told him about her new shoes, and how she might become a famous violinist who wore a long dress and bowed while people threw roses. Dad was such a good listener. Mom said he could listen till the cows came home, which meant forever, since zero cows lived here.

"Hey!" Cody suddenly realized something. "My hand doesn't itch anymore!"

"That's good."

"Only, Dad? Where'd the poison go?"

"Vanished into thin air, I guess."

Cody squinted at the air in front of her. "The world has a lot of invisible stuff floating around," she said.

"It's true. Like this." He was quiet for a second. "Feel it?"

"What?"

"The invisible hug I'm giving you. Feel it?"

She did. She did.

6
The Spindle

Even kids who hate school love the first day. On the playground, everyone ran around, calling hello, giving hugs and fist bumps. Cody's friend Pearl raced over, her black hair flying. Pearl was a friend to all, but especially to Cody.

"Is this Spencer?" Pearl asked, out of breath.

"Hello to you, too," said Cody. "Yes, this is Spencer. Spencer, this is Pearl."

"He's so cute!" Pearl's voice did a squeal.

"He got the Spindle."

"Oh." Pearl put her hand over her heart. "I'm sorry."

Spencer dug his fists into his cheeks. This was not a fun thing to watch.

"I have an idea," Cody said. "I'll introduce you! I'll explain all about you, and then she'll have to be nice to you."

Maybe.

"Good luck!" called Pearl.

Inside, the school was first-day clean. Instead of melted crayons and alien lunch meat, it smelled like lemons and new books. Not a single sticky spot on the floor. Mrs. Spindle's room was down the end of the hall. *Nick-nick-nick* (Cody's new purple boots). *Drag-drag-drag* (Spencer's new brown shoes).

Mrs. Spindle stood by her desk holding a fistful of poison arrows. Or possibly sharp pencils. When she saw Cody, her face got a look of this-must-be-a-bad-dream.

"Wrong room, Cody! I promoted you, in spite of everything."

"I came to introduce my best friend, Spencer."

"Ah, Spencer." Mrs. Spindle set down the poison arrows and shook his hand. "Welcome."

"He's really smart," Cody said. "He takes forever to make up his mind, but it's worth it."

"I bet he can speak for himself," said Mrs. Spindle.

"He's not big in the talking department. But . . ."

"Thank you, Cody." Mrs. Spindle gave one of her famous firm nods. "You may go now."

"One more thing . . ."

But before she knew it, Cody was out in the hallway. Spencer was alone, in the clutches of the Spindle.

At recess, Cody couldn't find him. He'd gotten punished already? Even for the Spindle, this was going too far!

The rule was no coming inside unless you required stitches or had to go really, really bad. Cody jumped up and down and did some groaning till at last the recess lady said, "Oh, fine."

Cody tiptoed down the hallway. Her spying skill was definitely coming in handy. Peeking around the door, she saw Mrs. Spindle and Spencer snipping shapes from construction paper. Both had their feet crossed at the ankle, and what do you know? Mrs. Spindle's brown shoes were the lady version of

Spencer's. Both of them liked the kind of plain, sensible shoes that made Mom shake her head and sigh.

Music was playing. Violin-y music.

A person who didn't know better would take this for a cozy, contented scene. Instead of jail.

"Whatever he did, he didn't mean it!" Cody marched to the front of the room. "Spencer never breaks rules on purpose! Keeping him in isn't fair!"

Spencer and Mrs. Spindle made twin faces of surprise. Mrs. Spindle set down her scissors.

"Cody, did you forget all those conversations we had about Thinking Before Speaking?"

Why did people keep asking if she forgot something? In the silence, violin music skipped all around the room.

"Cody?" said Mrs. Spindle.

"I am thinking before I speak."

"Good." Mrs. Spindle stood up. If she was a candy, she would be sugar-free. "Spencer's not in trouble. He and I are just getting to know each other. But you are right."

Cody jiggled her finger in her ear.

"Run along, dear," Mrs. Spindle told Spencer. "Fresh air is tonic for both mind and body."

"*Dear?*" said Cody when they were outside. "She calls you *dear?*"

"Mozart is her favorite, just like me."

Before Cody could say *Who-zart?*, Pearl ran up to them. Pearl was famous for origami, and now she handed Spencer an origami Yoda.

"I made it just for you. For a welcome present."

"Thanks," said Spencer.

Cody wiggled her eyebrows in a hello-did-you-forget-to-make-me-an-origami way, but somehow Pearl didn't notice.

After school, Mrs. Pickett walked them home. Till their new business got off the ground, she was going to watch Cody in the afternoons.

"How was your day?" she asked Spencer.

"He has the school's strictest teacher," Cody explained. "She's a legend in her time."

Mrs. Pickett's mouth did a twitch.

"But don't worry," Cody went on. "I introduced him, and then I rescued him. I'll stick to him like glue!"

"Thank you, Cody. That's very thoughtful of you," said Mrs. Pickett. "But let's not forget something."

Now what?

"Spencer needs to learn to take care of himself. That's one of his goals in his new school. Right, Spence?"

Spencer was still thinking this over when they got to GG's. A bush covered with pink, foamy flowers grew near the front steps. The bubble-bath bush, Cody called it. She gave it a tender pat, the way she always did, but today something caught her eye. Something shiny and pointy, poking out from underneath. Bending down, Cody pulled out a sword.

"Look at this!" She showed Spencer. "A pirate sword!"

"It's not real," he said.

"Probably it's a training sword, for beginner pirates."

"Better put it back," he said. "It might be someone's precious possession."

Finders keepers, losers weepers, said one side of Cody's brain. *Think how you'd feel if someone stole your precious possession,* said the other side. The two sides had a little boxing match — *bop! pow! thunk!*

Spencer stood there waiting. Cody sighed and slid the sword back under the bubble-bath bush. That boy had patience to spare. He could open a Patience Store and sell his extra patience.

7
Eraser Eater

"There's two more new kids!" Spencer said the next day at recess.

"That's nice," said Cody.

"No, it's not! One ate my eraser." He held up a pencil with a bald head. Then he pointed across the playground. "There they are!"

The girls had hair the color of a wildfire. One was a little bigger than Cody, and the other was a little smaller than Spencer. He ducked behind Cody, as if the eraser eater might take a bite of him.

"I told her rubber is bad for you," he said. "But she says she has a rare kind of stomach."

"Everybody out of our way!" the big girl said. "Unless you want a knuckle sandwich!"

She scrambled to the top of the climber, then reached down to help the little one up too. They folded their arms. They turned their heads from side to side, like masters of all they surveyed.

Cody had never seen anything like it.

Pearl came over and peeked behind Cody.

"Hello," she said, waving at Spencer. "Yoo-hoo back there!"

"Hello to you too, Pearl," said Cody.

"Look, Spence." Pearl reached around her. "I made you an origami allosaurus."

Up on the climber, the big girl grabbed the little one's hand. They stood up. One, two, three — they leaped off the tip-top! Spencer threw his hands over his eyes.

"That is so dangerous," he said. "That is extremely against the rules!"

"I know!" said Cody. Secretly, she'd always wanted to do it.

"They're just showing off," said Pearl. Someday she was going to make an excellent grown-up. "The best thing is to ignore them."

"What if she eats something else?" Spencer peeked through his fingers. "What if she eats my new crayons?"

"I'm pretty sure she'd puke all over the place," said Pearl.

Spencer moaned and hid behind his hands again.

After school, Cody and Spencer sat on GG's porch swing, with MewMew in between them. MewMew was special for many reasons, including the way her fur made her initial, M, above her eyes. This was her secret purring spot. When Cody rubbed it, MewMew revved up like a furry blender.

Swing, swing, swing. Purr, purr, purr. Spencer preferred his swinging slow and steady. So did MewMew.

After a long hard day at school, even Cody did. She slid off her sparkly purple boots, which, to tell the truth, were a little pinchy. She wiggled her toes. She'd said it before and she'd say it again. If you wanted peaceful and cozy, come to GG's.

"Cowabunga!"

The Meen door swung open. Cody could not believe her own naked eyes. Out came Eraser Eater and her little sister.

"What are you doing here?" E.E. demanded.

"He lives here," Cody said. "And I'm getting kid-sitted. What are *you* doing here?"

"Allow me to introduce ourselves. I am Molly Meen. And this is my trusty sidekick, Maxie Meen."

"You mean . . . ?" Spencer swallowed hard. "You mean you live next door to me?"

"That's what I mean, all right."

"But I don't get it," said Cody. "Where have you been?"

"I thought you'd never ask. I, Molly Meen, was at assassin school. And Maxie was at an international spy conference. Speak to them in Norwegian, Maxie."

"Blecca malecca!" said Maxie.

Spencer adjusted his glasses. He shook his round head. But Cody attempted a smile of friendship.

"Welcome back," she said. "By the way, I still have your father's jar of Big Ralph's meat tenderizer. I'll bring it back tomorrow."

Big Ralph's did not interest Molly Meen. She folded her arms and tapped her foot.

"From now on, this porch is off-limits for you," she said.

"That's not fair," Cody said. "This porch is half Spencer's."

"Not anymore! And you better not go in the backyard, either, if you know what's good for you. Tell them in Siberian, Maxie."

"Ooshka neva so!"

"Our father is an exterminator," said Molly. "Do you feel like getting exterminated?"

"This is against the law!" Cody said. "It's not fair!"

"All's fair in love and war!"

Molly grabbed her little sister, and they disappeared inside.

Spencer and Cody stared at each other.

They were not in love with the Meens, that was for sure.

So it must be war.

8
The P Word

Over the next few days, GG's house got cozier by the minute.

Mr. and Mrs. Pickett set up their business office in the dining room. They moved in computers, printers, telephones, folders, binders, and charts. Next to GG's Jackson Five poster, they hung one that said, "If you really want something, you will make it happen. If you don't, you will make excuses."

Anytime you opened a closet, something interesting fell out. GG's teacher stuff got all mixed up with

Spencer's kid stuff. Sometimes when she did her tai chi, GG accidentally stomped a Hot Wheels. Sometimes when Spencer climbed into his sleeping bag, he found MewMew curled up inside.

Another thing that made the house cozy, or possibly a tiny bit crowded, was that Cody and Spencer stayed indoors. All the time. No matter what.

Meanwhile, the Meens roller-skated from one side of the porch to the other, waving their pirate swords. They worked on a huge hole in the backyard. Every now and then, they peered in the window where Spencer and Cody watched. They crossed their eyes and wiggled their fingers in their ears.

"Why are you inside?" GG asked them. "It's a bee-yoo-tiful afternoon! Why don't you go play with the girls next door? They look like they could use some friends."

Spencer and Cody traded looks. If they told GG that eraser-eating, sword-waving pirates had declared war on them, she'd say, *Oh, for heaven's sake, just go make friends!* Because grown-ups, even smart ones like GG, can forget that making friends isn't always easy. Which was a big thing to forget, in Cody's opinion.

"We can't go out there," Cody said.

"Why on earth not?" GG said.

"Because . . ." Cody scrounged her brain. "Because Spencer is giving me a violin lesson!"

Spencer looked like he just swallowed something sharp and pointy. But he nodded and took out his violin.

"You have to be careful," he told Cody.

"I know that very well," she said.

"Don't forget."

"Grr."

Spencer explained how to hold the violin under your chin and crook your elbow in a way that gave you arm kinks after two seconds. He rubbed the bow with the special golden resin. He demonstrated how to draw it across the strings. Just when Cody thought he would never stop explaining, he did.

Her fingers tingled with excitement. She closed her eyes, just like Spencer when he played. She drew a deep breath. She lifted the bow.

Screeech!

Her eyes flew open. Spencer's hands were over his ears.

"Was that MewMew?" Cody asked. "Did she get in a catfight?"

"That was you!"

Cody's face grew warm. Something had gone wrong. All right. She would try again. She lifted the violin. She gripped the bow. She closed her eyes, took a deep breath and . . .

Screeech!

GG rushed into the living room. "Oh!" she said, puffing. "I wondered what that noise was!"

Cody itched like when the yellow jacket stung her, only all over. Instead of yellow-jacket poisoning, she had embarrassment poisoning.

"Don't feel bad," Spencer said. "I sounded even worse when I started."

Cody didn't believe that. But it was nice of him to say.

"Spencer practices every day," said GG. "Nobody learns the violin overnight. It takes a lot of . . ."

The word she said next began with a *p,* and it was

not *penguin*. Not *pizza* or *potato*, either. Cody sighed. She and GG sat on the couch, and Spencer played for them. That big fat show-off! Cody folded her arms. Her face wrinkled up like she had a mouthful of Extreme Sour Warheads.

But then, what do you know? That sneaky music snuck inside her. Today it was a razzle-dazzle kind of song, like dragonflies darting over sparkly water. Some people are scared of dragonflies, but not Cody. She thought they were fascinating.

Before she knew it, her sourness vanished into thin air. When Spencer bowed, she and GG stomped their feet and clapped. When they stopped, they heard a clapping echo. Cody looked out the window. The porch was empty, but the bubble-bath bush rustled in a strange and mysterious way.

Yes, mysterious.

9
The Baton of Love

Saturday was always the best day. But this one was extra best, because when Cody woke up, Dad was home!

She rushed into his arms and breathed in his Dad-ness. He put his ten-gallon hat on her head, and together they made pancakes. Cody cracked eggs with a flick of the wrist, the way he had taught her. She told him how she'd decided not to become a famous violinist after all, and Dad said she'd be a famous something, don't you worry.

In this life, many things are delicious, but Family Breakfast tops the list. Even Wyatt the Lovesick cheered up enough to eat a big stack. And then another big stack.

After Dad drove Mom to work, he and Cody did some cartoon watching. Wyatt was too old for cartoons, but what do you know? He watched, too. Not that he cracked a single smile.

"P.U. is being mean to Wyatt again," Cody told Dad in a low voice. Only not low enough.

"*Silencio,*" hissed Wyatt.

"Growing up is complicated," said Dad. "It's like driving a mountain road, full of twists and turns. Sometimes you're just hanging on to the edge. Other times, you can't believe how beautiful the view is."

"Like violin music," Cody said. "Is it happy? Is it sad? Maybe both?"

Wyatt did some soft groaning.

• • •

That afternoon, Dad took them apple picking. Cody was learning the times tables, and she recited the threes. Then she and Dad sang "You Are My Sunshine." In the backseat, Wyatt did more soft groaning. They were almost to the orchard when his phone rang.

"Yo!" he said.

Then, "You do?"

Then, "If you want!"

Then, "Okay."

By the time he hung up, Groaning Wyatt was Grinning Wyatt. If he was a candy, he'd be Pop Rocks.

"Let me guess," said Cody. "P.U. likes you again."

"None of your business," he said with a smile.

At the orchard, Wyatt boosted Cody up to reach the most perfect apples. He pretended he didn't want his whole caramel apple and let her finish it. And when a yellow jacket landed on it and Cody screamed, he didn't call her a wimpy crybaby. Instead he shooed it away, risking his own personal self. If there was a book called *The Perfect Big Brother*, guess who'd be on the cover?

"I noticed something funny," Cody told Dad. "When Payton Underwood is nice to Wyatt, Wyatt is nice to me."

"Hmm." Dad pushed back his cowboy hat and scratched his head. "I think you're on to something, Little Seed."

"But why? What's that hard-hearted girl got to do with me?"

Dad opened the car door, and they put their apples inside.

"Well, now," said Dad, "this is just a guess. It's been a century or two since I was a teenager. But I bet it's how special she makes him feel. That feels so nice, Wyatt can't keep it inside. He's got to pass the good feelings on."

"Like when we run relays in gym?" said Cody.

"Just like that!" Dad grinned. "Only instead of passing a baton, you pass the love."

The car smelled cider-sweet as they drove to pick up Mom from O'Becker Department Store. She was wearing her leopard-print skirt and golden gladiator sandals, Cody's favorite outfit. When she got in the car, she and Dad did a ginormous hello kiss.

Back home, Mom peeled, Dad sliced, Wyatt stirred, and Cody tasted. That applesauce came out perfecto, not a single lump. It was the best they'd ever made. It was the best times four.

"Group hug!" said Cody.

Wyatt made an escape attempt, but everybody ganged up on him. One long, sweet, cinnamon-y hug, that's what they had.

And that's how good things were, all weekend long.

10
Left Out

Monday morning, Cody could only find one purple boot. Then she could only find one polka-dot sneaker. Plus Wyatt had gotten up first, so when she poured her cereal, all that came out was dust.

Dad walked her to school. He had to leave again that afternoon, to haul more rocking chairs up from North Carolina. People sure did love rocking chairs. He turned his arms into a rocking chair and tipped Cody back and forth till she couldn't stop laughing.

Setting her back down, he said, "What's that on your foot?" He crouched down and fussed over her old broken-down sneakers.

Then it was time for their final This-Is-It Hug. Dad walked away backward, waving till she couldn't see him anymore.

Cody slumped on the edge of the playground. She watched the kindergartners lining up, even though the bell hadn't rung yet. They were so little, they still thought lining up was fun. They were so little, it was amazing their backpacks didn't topple them backward. Watching them gave Cody a tender twang. To think she'd once been that little and helpless herself.

Uh-oh. Speaking of helpless.

Cody had had such a nice weekend, she hadn't thought about Spencer at all. He'd been alone and at the mercy of the Means.

It was true! She did forget things. Important

things, like her best friend. Where was he? She looked all around the playground. She needed to tell him she was sorry — if he was still alive.

"Yoo-hoo!" Pearl waved. "Cody! Over here!"

She and Spencer were sitting on a bench. Spencer looked perfectly fine. But looks can fool you.

"I'm teaching Spencer to do origami," said Pearl.

"Are you all right?" Cody asked him. "Did the Means torture you all weekend?"

"They weren't there."

"What? They disappeared again?"

Spencer nodded. He held up his origami, which looked like a piece of paper he just pulled out of a wastebasket.

"Pretty good," Pearl said in her friend-to-all way. "You just need to practice."

"They disappeared again?" Cody couldn't believe it. "Do you know where?"

Spencer shrugged. He started folding another

piece of paper as Pearl made a face of encourage-
ment. Cody wiggled her way onto the bench between
them.

"You don't know? You don't have a clue? They
just vanished into thin air?" Cody waved her hands.
"They probably went for advanced assassin spy
training! Maybe in Siberia!"

"Cody"—Pearl's eyebrows shot up like fuzzy
drawbridges—"are you trying to stir something up?"

What?

"Excuse me, Pearl," Cody said. "I hate to say
it, but you are forgetting something. I know those
Meens better than you do. And I know Spencer *much,
much* better."

"I know that," said Pearl. "But there's no need
to . . ." She mouthed the next words so Spencer
wouldn't hear: *scare him.*

Whoa. Who did Pearl think she was? Spencer was
Cody's friend first, last, and always! But when she

looked at him, happily folding another terrible frog, her already heavy heart grew heavier. How could she forget about him all weekend? He could have been in mortal danger. What kind of friend acts like that? Hint: not a good one.

Pearl helped Spencer make his frog's head look more like a head. Cody sat between them, but she felt left out. She felt like she wasn't even there. Her own human head became a rock. A rock so big, her neck couldn't hold it up. *Donk*. Her head hung down. Cody stared at her old beat-up sneakers.

But wait. What was on the toes? She bent to look.

YOU ARE said her left foot. MY SUNSHINE said the right one.

Dad! That sneaky Pete! He must have written that, just before he left!

Tenderness bloomed inside her, like a garden in the sunshine. Dad liked her. No. He loved her. Cody could always count on that, no matter what.

"Gribbit!"

Cody looked up. A mutant frog hopped onto her knee.

"It's for you," said Spencer.

Her inside garden burst into full, gorgeous bloom. All at once, she didn't feel angry. Or left out. She took the frog and made him hop onto Pearl's knee. Pearl fed him a juicy invisible fly.

The baton of friendship, that's what it was. Passing from one to another.

11
The Fort

That afternoon, things were unnaturally peaceful at GG's. Nervous, Cody and Spencer checked around.

Behind the bubble-bath bush?

No.

In the garage?

No.

Down the backyard hole?

N-O spells *no*.

Maybe Molly and Maxie were on a special exterminating mission to Siberia or Norway. Maybe they wouldn't come back for a long time. Or ever. A person could hope.

Cody and Spencer took their peanut-butter-and-marshmallow sandwiches outside and sat in GG's butterfly chairs. The yard was so nice! A few yellow-gold leaves drifted down. The sky was deep blue. When you closed your eyes, the sun made Fourth-of-July sparklers on your lids.

"Let's tell riddles," said Cody. "What do frogs eat on hot summer days?"

"I give up."

"Hopsicles!"

Spencer laughed.

"Where do sheep go for a haircut?" Cody said.

"I give up."

"The baa-baa shop."

One of the many lovable things about Spencer was how he laughed. It took him a while to get going, but once he did, stand back. He would laugh so hard, his feet lifted right off the ground. It made you want

to poke him in the belly and, oops, Cody did! Before
you knew it, they were chasing each other around the
yard, zigging and zagging and stumbling and . . .

tumbling

down

into

the

hole.

Whoa. When those Meens dug something, they did not fool around.

"We could play dungeon down here," said Cody. "Or zombies rise from the grave."

"Or giant ants!" Spencer put his hands on his head and wiggled his fingers. "Giant radioactive ants, with antennas the size of baseball bats."

"Do we use our powers for good or evil?"

Spencer tapped his lip, thinking it over. And guess what? Cody waited patiently. Because this was exactly how she imagined things would be when he moved here. Making up cool games! Eating endless marshmallows! Having fun together every single minute!

"I vote for evil," said Spencer at last.

"Me too!" cried Cody. "Evil radioactive ants destroy the universe!"

"Evil?" boomed a voice from above. "Did I hear someone say evil?"

Spencer and Cody craned their necks. Mr. Meen loomed over them. From down in the hole, he looked bigger than Paul Bunyan.

"Sorry." Cody gasped. Her mouth went desert dry. "We were just leaving."

She scrambled out, but Spencer needed help. *Zoop!* Mr. Meen's muscle arm shot out and lifted him like a boy of feathers. Frowning, Mr. Meen plucked something off Spencer's shoulder and squeezed it between his big fingers.

"Red ant! Those dudes can bite." He flicked it away. "Too bad my girls aren't here. They could use some nice playmates like you."

Spencer and Cody traded looks. Could he possibly be talking about the same kids?

"Excuse me," said Cody. "But are your kids Molly and Maxie?"

"You already know them?" Mr. Meen grinned. His gold teeth made this a dazzling experience. "Great! I'll tell them you were playing in their fort."

"No!" cried Cody. "Please don't tell them!"

"What? You don't want to play with them?"

In this life, there are many surprises. One is that even men with pirate beards and gold teeth can look disappointed.

"Oh, well. They have colds, so they stayed an extra day at their mother's." Mr. Meen tugged at his cap. "They stay there weekends and summers, too."

"Does their mother live in Norway?" Spencer asked.

"You kids have great imaginations!" said Mr. Meen, and headed for the house.

The next day, Spencer brought his violin to school. Mrs. Spindle wanted him to try out for the orchestra. He was nervous, even though Cody told him the orchestra was awful and he was exactly what it needed.

Somebody lay in wait beside the flagpole. Make that two somebodies.

"You trespassed in our fort!" yelled Molly. "You must pay the penalty."

Maxie spoke not a word. Probably because she was busy sucking her thumb. And staring at Spencer's violin.

"Prepare to perish," said Molly. "Tell them in Hungarian, Maxie."

But Maxie couldn't take her eyes off the violin. Suddenly Cody was gifted with mind-reading powers. Maxie wanted to get her hands on it. She wanted to make beautiful music, too. Little did she know how hard it was. How much *p* word was required.

"Stop giving my sister the skunk eye!" Molly cried.

"You know," said Cody, "just because your name is Meen, you don't have to be."

"That's right!" said Molly. "We don't have to be! We *want* to be! Right, Maxie?"

But Maxie just sucked her thumb. When she wasn't throwing dirt bombs or yelling in Siberian, you could see that she was pretty small. Even smaller than Spencer. Hardly bigger than a fire hydrant.

"Right, Maxie? Maxie! Say something."

Maxie pulled her thumb out with a little pop.

"Are we going to Mommy's today?" she asked. "Or Daddy's?"

"Neither! We're going to advanced warrior training!"

Molly spun around, doing kicks and chops. Spencer covered his eyes.

12
Precious Possession

By now, GG's house was so cozy, a person could hardly turn around.

Mr. and Mrs. Pickett had business meetings in the dining room. Spencer's leaf project took over the kitchen table. It was a check-plus project, for sure. Pretty much everything Spencer did, the Spindle gave him a check-plus. Or even a check-plus-plus. Spencer said he was having an excellent experience in her class. This was a puzzle, all right. What had gotten into that teacher? Why was she so much nicer than last year?

Meanwhile, GG kept saying she loved having everyone live with her. Just loved it! Of course it wasn't getting on her nerves! What gave anybody that silly idea?

The whim-whams. Cody recognized the whim-whams when she saw them.

"How about some tai chi?" she said.

She and GG did Separating the Clouds and Rowing the Boat in the Middle of the Lake. They did Cody's favorite, Gazing at the Moon, which made you feel strong and graceful at the same time.

"Feel that *chi* flow through you," murmured GG. "From the top of your head to the tips of your toes!"

MewMew rolled on her back and tucked up her paws. This was cat tai chi.

"Feel the energy! Experience the mind-body harmony!"

Cody's insides got warm and peppy, like she just ate ten atomic fireballs. *Chi* was invisible to the naked eye, but it was there, all right. Could you see it under a microscope?

Cody asked Wyatt as he walked her home.

"What?" he said.

Cody asked him again.

"What?" he said.

Cody sighed. "P.U. gave you the brush-off again, didn't she?"

"What?" he said.

So it was true.

At home, Wyatt bent over his microscope. Cody studied her brother's neck. Mostly you don't think about your neck, but where would a person be without it? A neck has such an important job, but hardly anyone appreciates it. Plus, Cody noticed now, Wyatt's neck was awfully scrawny. She gave it a small, good-job pat.

"I'm sorry Payton dropped the love baton," she said.

"What are you talking about? No, never mind! I don't want to know!"

Cody heaved a sigh. "I'm so tired of people being mean."

"What?" Wyatt spun around. "Is someone being mean to you? Besides me, I mean?" He flexed his beginner muscles. "They better not! Not if they know what's good for them!"

Cody threw her arms around his trusty, scrawny neck. She breathed in his Wyatt-ness, a combination of anti-pimple soap, chocolate milk, and old socks. Wyatt let her do that for a whole five seconds before he peeled her off.

Of course Spencer got into the orchestra. The orchestra teacher even invited him to do a solo in the fall concert.

"Pearl is going to accompany me," he told Cody over the phone.

"She's going to walk you up to the stage?" That was so silly, it cracked Cody up.

"She's going to play the piano with me." Spencer

sounded happy. He sounded as happy as a boy who had just won a lifetime supply of candy and whose parents had never heard the words *tooth decay*. "It's called a duet."

"I know that!" said Cody. Well, now she did.

"We'll need to practice. I'll have to go over to her house."

"I can come with you," said Cody. "To make sure you don't get lost on the way."

"Cool. You can be our audience."

"Yeah. Cool."

Everyone knows being the audience is not as cool as being the one people clap for.

Cody went outside to visit the ants. She lay on her tummy. The ground was chilly. Winter was coming, and soon the ants would go inside their colony and not come out again till spring. What did they do down there all those months? Did they ever get the whim-whams? Did they do ant tai chi? In that fable, the grasshopper played a violin, but not the ants.

Whatever they did for entertainment, Cody was sure they clapped for one another. That's how ants were.

She crumbled up some crackers for their supper. They got straight to work, dragging crumbs. Mrs. Spindle would approve of how hard the ants worked, Cody thought. The ants were in favor of the same things as the Spindle was—no messing around, lots of cooperation.

All at once, Cody sat up. Maybe Mrs. Spindle wasn't actually nicer this year. Maybe . . . maybe she just liked Spencer. Maybe she liked him better than she did Cody!

Cody wrapped her arms around her knees. The ground beneath her felt really cold now. The problem with thinking was that sometimes your brain went places you did not want to follow.

An ant skedaddled across YOU ARE. Cody rested her chin on her knees. Well, she thought. Well, she liked Spencer, too. So she and Mrs. Spindle had something in common. You could even say they were a little bit alike.

Whoa. Who knew her brain was going to go *there*?

"Cody Louise!" Mom called from the house. "It's time for supper!"

Cody stood up carefully. She didn't want to jostle her brain, which suddenly seemed like a precious possession.

13
Asleep on the Job

A few days later, Cody's brain took her someplace else. Only this time, that place was called Trouble.

After school, Spencer went to Pearl's house to practice their duet, and guess who was not invited? Guess who wound up sitting all by herself in GG's living room, surrounded by Spencer stuff but no Spencer?

"They'll be practicing," said Mrs. Pickett. "It wouldn't be much fun for you."

A sticky note was stuck to Mrs. Pickett's elbow. She looked like she'd forgotten about a thing called brushing your hair. She and Mr. Pickett were almost ready to launch, which sounded like they had a boat or a rocket ship, but no. Their business, that's what they were launching.

"You just make yourself at home, sugar. He'll be home before you know it." Mrs. Pickett hurried back to the dining room/office.

Cody and MewMew waited by the window. For MewMew, waiting equaled sleeping, but for Cody, waiting equaled torture. Outside, the afternoon sun shone bright. *Come out, come out,* called the day.

No sign of a Meen.

Cody opened the front door and tiptoed over to the swing. Just as she sat down, a car pulled up to the curb. Molly, Maxie, and a woman climbed out. Cody slid down and spied through the porch railing.

The woman's hair had a pretty purple streak, and

her arms were covered with beautiful tattoos. She pulled Molly and Maxie close. What do you know! Those Meens were expert huggers. But when Tattoo Woman tried to go, Maxie wouldn't let her.

"Not yet, Mommy!" Maxie attached herself like a bear cub on a tree. "We didn't do One Last Time."

So they did more hugging, then some tickling. Maxie still wouldn't let go. Hiding on the porch, Cody's eyes prickled. Saying good-bye to your parent was always so hard. Even when you were as big as Cody, it was hard. Just think how Maxie felt.

As their mother climbed into the car, Maxie looked ready to cry. But quick quick, Molly boosted her little sister onto her back. She piggybacked Maxie around in circles. Instead of crying, Maxie started giggling.

Aw. That was so nice. It was exactly the kind of thing good old Wyatt would do to cheer her up. Cody jumped to her feet.

"I love your mother's tattoos!" she called. "Is she a tattoo artist? Do you guys have tattoos, too?"

Molly spun around. So much for her smile.

"You spied on us!" she yelled.

Asleep on the job, that was Cody's brain. How could it forget these were her mortal enemies?

Molly was no forgetter. She was a champion rememberer.

"Plus you're trespassing on our territory! That is a double violation!"

Before she knew what she was doing, Cody threw her arms over her head.

"Can you do this?" she said. "It's called Gazing at the Moon."

What in the world? said Molly's face. But Maxie tried it.

"Very good!" said Cody. "Now try this one. It's called Rowing the Boat in the Middle of the Lake."

Mr. Meen stepped out onto the porch.

"What's going on out here, a dance party?" he cried. "Why wasn't I invited?"

Suddenly he frowned. He lifted his boot and smashed it back down.

"Dang spiders," he said.

Molly climbed the steps. She pointed at the

squished spider. Then at Cody. Then back at the
spider.

Cody lifted her chin. She tried for a smile that said,
Ha! You think you scare me? Think again!

But the best she could manage was fake cheeri-
ness, like someone on a hand sanitizer commercial.

You might think that after so much trouble, tomorrow would be a better day, but sorry. You would be
wrong.

14
Crime Scene

Right after morning meeting, Cody's teacher said to clear desks for the spelling test. She couldn't believe her ears. Test? Today?

One of the words was *alligator*. That was a hard one, even if you remembered to study. How many *l*'s? Was it *e* or *o*? She drew a cute little alligator, to make up for getting it wrong.

After that, gym. Cody was wearing her YOU ARE MY SUNSHINE sneakers, like every day since Dad left. But when she tried to double-knot them, the MY SUN-SHINE lace broke.

And when she ran, the shoe's tongue flapped.

And when she tripped and bumped heads with Dimitri, whoa. Who knew skulls were that hard?

The gym teacher sent them to the nurse. The nurse made them hold ice packs till they got brain freeze. It was Pizza Day, but by the time Cody and Dimitri got to the lunch room, the pizza was cold. Cody had ordered two slices of pepperoni, but only plain was left.

The lunch lady felt bad and gave them double chocolate milks.

Something nice to know: even lunch ladies have soft spots.

Spencer and Pearl were sitting together. Down at the end of the table, Molly was sitting by herself. She looked tired. She gave a big yawn. No gold teeth.

"What are you looking at?" she said to Cody.

"Nothing!"

"I was up late watching *The Revenge of Bog Man*."

"You were?" Cody had begged her head off to watch that movie, but Mom said absolutely not. "Was Bog Man all oozy? Did he leave a trail of repulsive green slime?"

"Oh, yeah! But the coolest part was when he . . ." Molly stopped. Her eyes turned to slits. "Hey. You're not trying to be my friend, are you?"

"No! No way!"

"Good." Molly got busy tearing her pizza crust into smithereens.

Cody sat down with Spencer and Pearl. Pearl stuck a piece of crust on her nose.

"Guess what I am," she said.

"Pinocchio," Cody said.

"No," Pearl said.

"A narwhal," Spencer said. "Which is the unicorn of the sea."

"Right!" Pearl said.

Cody sighed. She opened both milks at once and put the straws in.

"Dimitri cracked my brain," she said. "In case anybody cares."

She took a slurp of chocolate milk times two. Down at the end of the table, Molly gave her the skunk eye. Cody shifted on her seat. Across the table, Spencer and Pearl blabbed about the orchestra. Cody shifted some more. And then somehow her bungie slipped off the back. Cody grabbed for the table but, whoa! She was on her way down. The milk cartons

were on their way up. They somersaulted through the air.

When Cody got back on her feet, Spencer and Pearl were flapping their arms and squawking. They had chocolate milk all over them.

Not only them. The table. And the wall. And the floor.

It was like a TV crime scene, only with chocolate milk instead of blood.

Cody got napkins. She said sorry sorry sorry. But a laugh tickled her insides. Not laughing is extremely hard, as hard as not crying. Cody tried to keep that laugh inside, but it's possible a tiny bit leaked out.

"I do not find this situation funny," said Pearl.

But someone else did. Down at the end of the table, that someone gave Cody the thumbs-up. Which from a normal person would be a good thing, but who knew what it meant coming from Molly Meen?

That night, Mom brought home new shoelaces. She pulled out the old broken ones and threaded in a deluxe, sparkly pair. She slipped the sneakers onto Cody's feet and tied professional bows.

"These shoes are too small. You've got no room in the toe box." Mom smiled. "But they're stunning on you, madam."

The shoes were perfect now. Part old, part new. Part Dad, part Mom. Cody curled up her toes to stop them from growing any more.

"Those shoes remind me of that song, 'Make new friends, but keep the old,'" said Mom.

She and Cody sang it together. A duet!

Cody ran upstairs to show Wyatt. He drooped across his bed. If he was a sandwich, he'd be a tuna melt. The phone was to his ear. One look and Cody knew who he was talking to. That old P.U.! Cody flopped on the bed beside him.

"Tell her unless she's nice to you, you won't be nice to her," she said.

"*What?*" Payton piped up on the other end. "What did you say?"

"Nothing!" Wyatt tried to get Cody in his famous Houdini headlock, but she wriggled away.

"Tell her all's not really fair in love and war," said Cody.

"What?" said Phone Payton.

"Go away!" said Wyatt.

"WHAT?" cried P.P.

"Not you!" he said.

Payton's voice got squeaky, like a hamster wheel in the middle of the night. Wyatt had to hold the phone away from his ear. *Squeak squeak,* went Payton. It sounded so funny, Cody wanted to laugh. Remember how hard it is to keep a laugh inside?

A corner of Wyatt's mouth went up. He pulled it down but *boing!* It curved right back up.

"What's so funny?" squeaked Payton.

"You. No! I mean—I mean—I gotta go, Payton."

"I'm not done talking!"

"Bye."

He clicked off.

Silencio.

Cody stopped laughing. She prepared for the Wrath of Wyatt. Her brother set the phone down. And then he heaved a sigh. A big sigh, like instead of a cell phone, he set down something that weighed a gazillion tons.

"You deserve to suffer a long and painful death," he told her.

Instead, he just put her in the headlock. Cody thought she heard him say, *"Gracias, amiga."* But it was hard to tell for sure, with her ears squished like that.

15
You Humans

Spencer and Pearl were practicing their duet again. They practiced so much, you'd think they were going to perform in the Super Bowl, instead of the school all-purpose room.

Cody kept busy helping Mr. and Mrs. Pickett. She learned which corner of the envelope the stamp goes on. Also how to fold a letter exactly into thirds. Which was as hard as origami, she bet.

"What a patient girl you are!" said Mrs. Pickett.

There is a difference between being patient and having no choice. But a wise voice inside Cody said, *Do not point this out.*

That night, she decided to pay Spencer a quick quick visit before supper. For once, the Meen side of the house was lit up, and GG's side was dark. Cody stood at the bottom of the front steps, wondering where they could be. Her heart jumped when a small voice spoke from the shadows.

"They're gone."

Maxie! She was sitting on GG's swing, eating a doughnut. It was Cody's favorite kind, with that chocolate icing you can pick off in pieces. Maxie had fake tattoos all over her arms. She wore her father's big exterminator boots with the steel tips.

But the biggest surprise of all was she had Mew-Mew in her lap.

"Where did they go?" Cody asked.

"Out to eat. I heard them saying, 'Chinese or Mexican?'"

Cody knew it was her duty to make Maxie hand over MewMew. Because who could trust a Meen? She might yank MewMew's tail at any moment!

But in this life, there are many surprises, and sometimes you surprise your own self. Cody sat down on the swing. She rubbed MewMew's secret spot. That cat purred like a miniature lawn mower. She purred so loud, Maxie laughed. And then, what do you know? Cody petted Maxie's little head instead of MewMew's.

"I like your tattoos," Cody said.

Maxie broke off a piece of doughnut and shared it with Cody.

Most of the chocolate icing fell onto the floor.

It was not exactly the baton of love.

But it was still nice.

"I like listening to his guitar," Maxie said.

"It's a violin. But me, too."

Swing, swing. They finished the doughnut. *Swing,*

swing. They listened to the slow, end-of-summer cricket song. *Swing, swing.*

Until the Meen door flew open and Molly catapulted onto the porch.

"Maxie, what are you doing? Did she brainwash you? Get away from her this second!"

Slowly Maxie got up. She handed MewMew to Cody. She slid her thumb, which was smaller than a baby carrot, into her mouth. *Shuffle, shuffle.* She crossed the porch in her father's boots.

"That's better," said Molly.

But no. It was not. It was not better at all. Inside Cody, something went *snap*. Something went, *That is enough!* She set MewMew down. She drew a deep breath and stood up.

"It's not better! It's way worse." She puffed out her chest. "I've had enough of this war. It's stupid! I'm sick of it!"

Molly opened her mouth, but nothing came out.

For about one second.

"What did you call us?"

"Not you! The war!"

"You called us stupid! We heard it with our own ears! Right, Maxie?"

Molly's hair flamed like a forest fire. Her eyes shot sparks. Cody went wobbly kneed. But she set her new-old, Mom-Dad shoes wide apart.

"Take it back!" said Molly. "Or else!"

"Or else what?"

"Or else . . . or else . . . Wait a minute."

Molly and Maxie held a conference. Meaning Molly did all the talking and Maxie nodded. At last Molly spun around.

"You're sick of this war, right?" she said.

"Right." Hopefulness bubbled up inside Cody.

"Then let's end it."

"Okay!"

"We'll have a fight to the finish!"

"Wait."

"Tomorrow!"

"Wait."

"Tomorrow, after school, it's showdown time for you and your scaredy-cat friend."

The door banged shut behind them.

Cody couldn't believe it. What had she gotten them into? How was she going to tell Spencer he was in a fight to the finish?

This was a disaster. A disaster times ten.

"Mew?" MewMew rubbed against her legs. This was cat for "What's wrong with you humans? Where did that little kid go? The one who was petting me so nicely and dropping delicious doughnut crumbs all over?"

Cody went down the porch stairs very slowly. At the bottom, she noticed something lying under the bubble-bath bush. Maxie's sneakers. One had a broken shoelace. *Twang* went Cody's heart.

She sat down on the bottom step. In this life,

humans are the only ones who can really talk. But sometimes it feels like other things can, too. Ants. Cats. Shoes.

Cody found a crayon in her pocket. She picked up the sneakers and got to work.

16
Big Boss

That night, Cody lay in bed listening to the *tap-tap-tap* of the rain on her window. In the daytime, that was a comfy sound. But at night, it was so lonesome.

Cody took Gremlin down the hall. Gremlin used to be Wyatt's, but now he was hers. Her brother was awake, too. This was a surprise, considering what a world-class sleeper he was. He lay with his arms under his head. Cody curled up next to him.

"Why aren't you asleep?" she said.

"Why aren't you?"

"It's complicated," she said.

"Tell me about it."

Tap-tap-tap went the rain. It didn't sound lonesome here in Wyatt's room.

"Wyatt?"

"Hmm."

"Everybody says fighting is bad." She hugged Gremlin tight. "But what if you can't help it?"

"Hmm." He rubbed his chin, just the way Dad did. "Sometimes you really can't help it. Like me and Payton. Sometimes you have to stand up for yourself, or else you're giving in. You're letting the bad stuff win."

"That's what I was thinking." She hugged Gremlin tighter.

"But you know what?" said Wyatt-Dad. "In the end, fighting doesn't solve anything. Because unless you work things out, somebody's stuck with bad feelings. The mean, rotten stuff doesn't really go away."

"Where does it go?"

Wyatt pooched his lips. "Good question," he said.

"Maybe it gets passed on. Like the baton of love. Only the opposite."

"This is getting scary. That almost made sense to me."

They lay there listening to the rain on the roof. Cody asked Wyatt if he'd like to have Gremlin back for tonight. But Wyatt said he was good.

"You need to get to sleep, okay?" he said.

"Okay."

And she did.

Worry. It's such a big boss. It bosses all the good feelings right out the window.

The next morning, Mrs. Pickett walked them to school holding the biggest cup of coffee Cody had ever seen. She and Mr. Pickett had pulled an all-nighter to get their website ready for the launch.

Spencer carried his violin and his amazing leaf

project. He looked so happy. He looked lit up from the inside out, like a lantern wearing glasses.

Cody decided to wait till later to tell him that in just a few hours, he was doomed to a fight to the finish.

The playground was nice and muddy. Kids ran around slipping and sliding. Cody rescued three worms stranded on the sidewalk and put them safely back in the grass. Molly Meen, Pirate Queen, pointed at them from the top of the climber.

"Don't forget!" she cried.

"Forget what?" said Spencer.

"Umm. I forget," said Cody.

Spencer gave her a strange look.

By the end of the day, Cody had the whim-whams. On the way to GG's, she tried to calm herself down by saying the four times table. The times tables were like a parade. When you wrote them, the numbers marched along in perfect straight lines. And when you said them out loud, they beat like a drum.

"Four times one is four! Four times two is eight!"

Mrs. Pickett kept yawning. Even her ears looked tired. Spencer told her to go take a little rest. He said he could make their snack.

"My big boy." His mother gave him a kiss. "I'm so proud of you. You really are learning how to take care of yourself!" Then she gave Cody a kiss, too, and up the stairs she went.

Spencer got out the crackers. He measured out perfectly equal amounts of apple juice. But no way Cody could eat.

"There's something I need to tell you," she said.

Before she could say another word, footsteps pounded up the back steps.

"Battle time!" yelled a familiar voice. "Don't even think about chickening out!"

Behind his glasses, Spencer's eyes popped.

"Escape is impossible!" yelled the voice. "The time is at hand!"

Footsteps pounding away.

"That," said Cody. "That's what I needed to tell you."

Spencer gripped the apple juice like it was trying to get away. "What's happening? What battle?"

"I couldn't help it," Cody said. "I got sick of them bossing us around!"

"You challenged them to a battle?"

"Not really. Just sort of."

Spencer set the juice down. He shook his big, round head.

"What were you thinking?" he said.

"Are you sure you don't have some secret fighting skills you never told me about?"

"We're going to get exterminated," Spencer said.

17
Fight to the Finish

Spencer curled into a Spencer ball. The boy who knew how to take care of himself was gone. Old, timid Spencer was back.

"I'm no good at fighting. Besides, fighting is bad! It just makes things worse."

"How can things get worse? We have to stand up for ourselves. Otherwise we let the bad stuff win."

"I don't want to get creamed," he whispered. "Getting creamed is not good, in my experience."

Spencer's eyes grew shiny with tears. He needed

Cody to protect him, all right. He needed her, the same as he used to.

Cody felt a tiny bit glad.

But just a tiny bit. Because right then, Cody understood something she didn't before.

She needed Spencer, too.

"We can do it together," she said. "Like the ants! If we stick together."

"I can't," said Spencer. And then, all of a sudden, he sat up straighter. "And I won't! You're the one who got us into this! I wasn't even here."

"I know! Because you keep going over to Pearl's."

"I can't help it if I have to practice."

"You and your dumb violin. You and dumb Pearl."

"*Dumb* is a mean word!"

"So?"

"So . . . go ahead and fight! I refuse."

Spencer crossed his arms on his chest. He squinched his eyes shut, like a little kid who thinks that if he can't see you, you can't see him.

"Fine!" Cody jumped up. "Be like that! You microscopic bacteria, you!"

She waited a minute, hoping Spencer would change his mind. But his eyes stayed shut. His arms stayed crossed. At last, she opened the door and stepped outside.

The backyard was soppy with puddles. A bird perched on GG's brimming birdbath.

No Meens in sight.

Cody stood very still. Please! Let Molly get sick of war, too. Let her sign a peace treaty. Please! Let . . .

Behind her the door creaked open. She spun around. Spencer!

"I knew it!" Cody hugged him. "I knew you'd stick with me!"

Really, she hadn't known it at all. But she'd hoped it. And that is just as good.

"Shh! They might be planning an ambush." Spencer swiveled his head. "They could be hiding, waiting to jump out."

"Unless they—"

"Cowabunga!"

Molly and Maxie charged up out of their hole. Well, Molly did. Maxie had to get hauled out. They'd plastered their faces with mud war paint. They waved their swords. They gave bloodcurdling battle cries.

Sometimes your feet are moving before your brain even knows it. Cody and Spencer took off, running as fast as they could. Only this was not very fast at all, because Spencer was always slow and the ground was one big mud-goosh. Cody gripped his hand.

Around the yard they went. First Cody dragging Spencer, then Molly, then, bringing up the rear, Maxie. Around and around they went, past GG's garden, the big hole, the butterfly chairs. Spencer started gasping for breath. He couldn't keep it up much longer. They had to do something. But what?

"Throw something!" Cody commanded.

He pulled off his sensible shoe. Like a mighty warrior, he swung it over his head and let go. It missed the Meens by about a mile.

"Throw something back!" Molly commanded.

Maxie pulled off her sneaker but slipped on the wet grass. Her arms shot out like a superhero who just lost her super flying power.

Whomp! Maxie landed on the ground.

Whomp, whomp! Her big sister landed on top of her. This was Cody and Spencer's chance to escape. They spun around and flew toward the house.

Except.

Another bloodcurdling scream.

"Yellow jackets!"

Cody looked back. Molly leaped to her feet, slapping the air around her. What Cody saw then turned her ice cold. Cold in parts of her she didn't even know could get cold.

Yellow jackets swarmed up from a hole in the ground. Not one. Not two or three or ten. Dozens and dozens, more than she could count. Grabbing Spencer, Cody started to run.

"Look out!" she yelled over her shoulder. "Get away! Quick!"

Molly ran, too. But not Maxie. She froze. She turned into a Maxie statue. The furious yellow jackets buzzed straight for her. War! They declared war against her for disturbing their nest!

"Maxie! Run for your life!"

But she just stood there, hypnotized. Cody's heart did a cartwheel. She remembered how bad her sting hurt. Bad bad bad! She raced back, picked Maxie up, and took off. She didn't stop till she was up the back steps and safe inside GG's kitchen.

Only, uh-oh.

By mistake, she'd run up the wrong steps.

This was the Meen kitchen.

"What's all the racket? What'd I tell you kids about playing nice?"

Steel-toed boots stomped toward them.

18
Stung

Cody had never been indoors with Mr. Meen before. The way a Christmas tree always looks bigger when you take it inside the house, so it was with Mr. Meen.

"Look at the mud you tracked in! I just scrubbed this floor!" But then he saw that Maxie was crying. "What happened? What have you kids been doing?"

The back door banged open. In rushed Molly and Spencer.

"Killer bees!" Molly's face matched her hair. "They attacked us!"

Something you might not know: even Pirate Queens cry.

"Dang bugs!" roared Mr. Meen. "Sit down! Show Daddy. Aw, I know it hurts, Max."

Another thing you might not know: all dads, even the exterminator ones, want to make their kids feel better.

And Mr. Meen turned out to be a feel-better expert. One two three, he had Maxie patched up and slathered with Big Ralph's. He had her blowing her nose in a napkin instead of her sleeve. Molly kept saying the bees got her, too, but even though Mr. Meen looked, he couldn't find a single sting.

"They didn't get you, honey pie," he said.

"Yes, they did! It really hurt!"

Mr. Meen flashed his dazzling, gold-toothed smile.

"Your baby sister got hurt. You're such a good sister, you felt her pain." He turned to Cody. "You didn't get stung again, did you?"

"Not this time."

"She saved me!" said Maxie. "She saved me from killer bees!"

"She did?" Mr. Meen smacked the table. "Now, that's what I call super brave. Because this is a girl who knows firsthand that a sting is no fun."

"That's how come I did it," said Cody. "I remembered how much it hurts."

"Well, the entire Meen family thanks you." He pumped her hand up and down. "You like ribs?"

"Huh?"

"Because I'm cooking up some tonight, and I got plenty." He slapped the table again. "Tell you what. Invite that nice old lady Grace, too. And those other two that are always running around like chickens with their heads chopped off. Let's celebrate you kids becoming friends at last!"

Molly's mouth made a shape like an egg. But Maxie . . . Well.

In this life, many things are sweet:

Marshmallows

A cat purring in your lap

Violin music played by someone who knows what he is doing

But nothing is sweeter than a little kid hugging you. Even one slathered with mud and meat tenderizer.

19
YOU ARE . . .

Mr. Meen, wearing an apron that said STAND BACK—DAD'S COOKING!, set up a table on the porch. GG brought out plates and napkins and her home-made green-tomato chutney. Mrs. Pickett stumbled out, rubbing her eyes, and a little later, Mr. Pickett got home from his meeting. Soon Mom and Wyatt arrived with a salad and a giant bag of chips.

Cody held the chips out to Molly and Maxie. Molly gave her a suspicious look. For two seconds.

"Oh, well. Don't mind if I do."

Maxie kept scratching her arms.

"You know why you itch?" Cody said. "Invisible poison."

"Are you trying to scare my little sister?" Molly set her hands on her hips.

"Actually, *my* sister's right." Wyatt stepped up. "You have been injected with a toxic venom of reactive peptides, invisible to the naked eye." He patted Maxie on the head. "Good news is, it'll go away."

Wyatt made a muscle. It was magnificent, like a knot in a skinny rope. Molly looked at it with eyes of respect. She ate another big handful of chips.

"Are those the kids who were mean to you?" Wyatt whispered, and Cody nodded. "They don't look so bad," he said. "Maybe you should let bygones be bygones."

Cody thought this over. Wasn't that the same thing as forgetting? The very thing people were

always scolding her for? Was there such a thing as *good*
forgetting? Whew. In this life, there is always something new to think about.

GG switched on her music. She grabbed Maxie's
hand and demonstrated the Loco-Motion. Before
you knew it, Mom and the Picketts were dancing,
too. Those grown-ups could get down! The porch

shivered and shook. This was probably the most humans it had ever seen in its entire porch life. Not a single person more could fit.

Wrong! Like those gloves that stretch to fit any hand, that's how that porch turned out to be. Because surprise—here came Dad, home early! And he fit just fine. Fine times a million!

133

Love always fits. GG said it was a scientific fact. Now she handed Cody a cookie.

"We never did get our welcome celebration, but this is even better!" GG winked. "Admit it, Cody Louise. Patience is a virtue."

"You know what else is a virtue? Wearing shoes." Mr. Meen pointed at Maxie's feet. Somehow she'd lost both shoes. "What did you do with yours this time?"

"I was about to ask you the same thing, Spence," said Mrs. Pickett.

"We'll find them," Cody said.

She and Spencer walked around to the backyard. Very carefully, utilizing yellow-jacket radar, they shoe-hunted. They circled the big hole. Cody wondered if Molly and Maxie would like to play evil radioactive ants in it. They looked under GG's butterfly chairs. She wondered if the four of them could sit here and have a winter picnic. She wondered if Molly ever loaned out her pirate sword.

Spencer's shoe was under a tomato plant. One of Maxie's lay nearby.

"Hey," he said, picking it up. "It says YOU ARE. That's funny. You are what?"

He hunted for the other one. How peaceful it was back here. The distant music from the porch mixed with the sound of one bird singing his bird family to sleep.

"Here it is!" cried Spencer.

Maxie's other shoe had landed in a mud puddle. Cody rubbed it clean with leaves and grass and, oops, her T-shirt. She set the two sneakers down side by side.

"'You are,'" read Spencer, "'not mean.'" He pushed his glasses up his nose. "You wrote that, didn't you?"

"Yup."

In the grass, two ants skedaddled by. Maybe they were headed for the party. Or maybe they wanted to get home before it was too dark. Overhead, the stars

were getting busy. One by one, they popped out, so
bright and sharp you could almost hear them. *Ping
ping ping!* Even in the daytime, when you couldn't
see them, the stars were there. Invisible, like so many
things in this complicated universe.

After a while, Cody and Spencer moseyed back to the music and food and laughing.

"Do you think the Meens will be nice to us now?" said Spencer.

"I was wondering the same thing."

"We'll have to be patient," said Spencer. "We'll have to wait and see."

But somehow Cody's impatient feet started running. She couldn't wait one more second to be with her family, and her friends, and the people who might possibly be her new friends. She couldn't wait to see what happened next. See it all with her own naked eye.

> **"Cody is perfectly charming
> and charmingly imperfect!"**
> —Sarah Pennypacker, author of the Clementine series

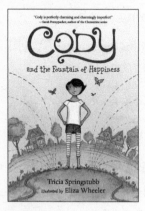

Before Spencer moved in for good and school started, there was summer vacation. With everyone busy and camp closed for the summer, how can Cody find her fountain of happiness?

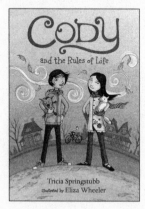

With Spencer and the Meen girls settled in to the neighborhood, Cody is ready for winter with her friends. But when Pearl trusts Cody with her favorite toys, Cody gets a crash course in the rules of life.